SKIPPER'S LOG

BY MICHAEL ANTHONY STEELE
ILLUSTRATED BY ARTFUL DOODLERS

GROSSET & DUNLAP
An Imprint of Penguin Group (USA) Inc.

nickelodeon **The PENGUINS of MADAGASCAR** ™

DreamWorks®

GROSSET & DUNLAP
Published by the Penguin Group
Penguin Group (USA) Inc., 375 Hudson Street, New York, New York 10014, USA
Penguin Group (Canada), 90 Eglinton Avenue East, Suite 700, Toronto,
Ontario M4P 2Y3, Canada (a division of Pearson Penguin Canada Inc.)
Penguin Books Ltd., 80 Strand, London WC2R 0RL, England
Penguin Group Ireland, 25 St. Stephen's Green,
Dublin 2, Ireland (a division of Penguin Books Ltd.)
Penguin Group (Australia), 250 Camberwell Road, Camberwell,
Victoria 3124, Australia (a division of Pearson Australia Group Pty. Ltd.)
Penguin Books India Pvt. Ltd., 11 Community Centre,
Panchsheel Park, New Delhi—110 017, India
Penguin Group (NZ), 67 Apollo Drive, Rosedale,
North Shore 0632, New Zealand
(a division of Pearson New Zealand Ltd.)

Penguin Books (South Africa) (Pty.) Ltd., 24 Sturdee Avenue,
Rosebank, Johannesburg 2196, South Africa

Penguin Books Ltd., Registered Offices: 80 Strand, London WC2R 0RL, England

Library of Congress Control Number: 2010002652

ISBN 978-0-448-45409-2   10 9 8 7 6 5 4 3 2 1

HOLD IT RIGHT THERE, CIVILIAN!

THIS OFFICIAL LOGBOOK IS TOP SECRET. I REPEAT, TOP SECRET! THE CONTENTS OF THIS BOOK ARE REVEALED ON A ''NEED TO KNOW'' BASIS AND BELIEVE ME, *YOU DON'T NEED TO KNOW.* SO IF THIS HIGHLY CLASSIFIED LOGBOOK SOMEHOW FELL INTO YOUR HANDS, DO THE RIGHT THING, MY FRIEND. RETURN IT TO PENGUIN HQ, CARE OF THE NEW YORK ZOO. TRUST ME . . . YOU DON'T WANT ME TO COME AND GET IT!

NOTE TO SELF:

THIS LOGBOOK REPLACES AN EARLIER VERSION THAT MYSTERIOUSLY VANISHED. FULL OF SENSITIVE PENGUIN INFORMATION, THE LAST LOGBOOK HAS, NO DOUBT, FALLEN INTO ENEMY HANDS. PERSONALLY, I SUSPECT MY MAD DOLPHIN NEMESIS, DR. BLOWHOLE. I WOULDN'T PUT ANYTHING PAST THAT MARINE MAMMAL FOE.

SKIPPER'S LOG

07:00 HOURS:

I AWOKE WITH A SPRING IN MY STEP, FINS READY FOR ACTION.

07:01 HOURS:

MY SURROUNDINGS SEEMED QUIET—*TOO* QUIET. I HAD BEST BE ON MY GUARD. BUT, THEN AGAIN, I WAS *ALWAYS* ON MY GUARD.

07:02 HOURS:

I INSPECTED THE INTERIOR PERIMETER. ONLY A SELECT FEW KNEW THAT THE PENGUIN ''HABITAT'' WAS REALLY THE TOP SECRET BASE OF AN ELITE STRIKE FORCE WITH UNMATCHED COMMANDO SKILLS.

07:05 HOURS:

I ROUSED THE MEN. ''UP AND AT 'EM, MEN!'' I SHOUTED. ''FALL IN FOR ROLL CALL!''

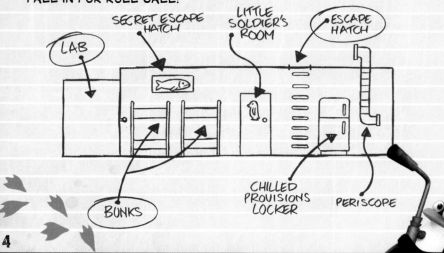

LAB

SECRET ESCAPE HATCH

LITTLE SOLDIER'S ROOM

ESCAPE HATCH

BUNKS

CHILLED PROVISIONS LOCKER

PERISCOPE

Name: Skipper
Rank: Skipper
Expertise: Leadership, courage in the face of danger, delegation skills
Status: Active

Skipper is commander of the elite penguin commando squad. There's a confident swagger in his waddle as he keeps a cool head during many dangerous situations. ~~An~~ *He's* strict but fair and keeps his troops running like a well-oiled machine. A role model and natural leader, his men look up to him with admiration and a certain sense of awe.

Skipper is a master in hand-to-fin combat. Yet he has never been afraid to incorporate more *eccentric* fighting styles. This comes as no surprise to anyone who has faced his top secret *corkscrew* maneuver. Skipper has no problem employing unconventional solutions to get the job done. After all, penguins are nature's rebels—they're birds who refuse to fly and swim instead. And Skipper is the finest example of this species. He's a penguin who will do whatever it takes to complete the mission. Even if it means breaking one or two of nature's so-called "laws."

SKIPPER

5

Name: Kowalski
Rank: Second-in-Command
Expertise: Tactical options, statistics, data analysis
Status: Active

When I need options, Kowalski has his clipboard ready and his brain on overdrive! When we need a custom-built scanner, rocket ship, or super ray, this penguin is there with empty sardine tins, duct tape, and a beak full of ingenuity.

A master tactician, Kowalski creates many of the team's top secret plans. He even came up with the *strategic retreat* maneuver (which is similar to running away but not as wimpy-sounding). Although Kowalski can hold his own in a fight, I'd take his brains over his brawn any day of the week. I count myself lucky to have a second-in-command who values science as much as a well-placed karate chop.

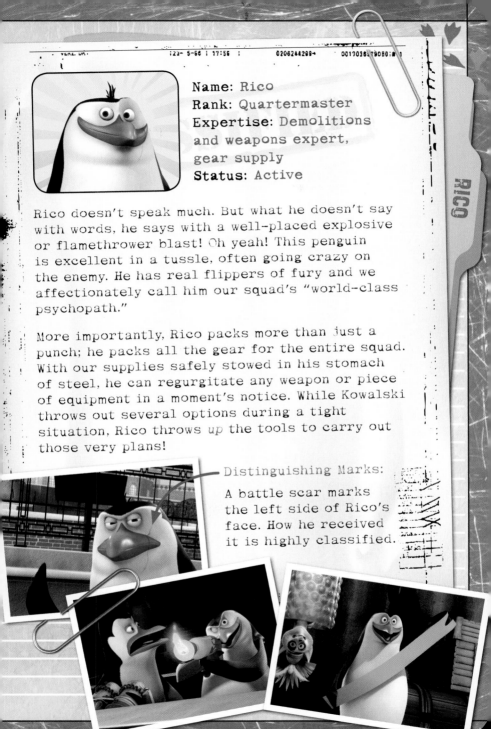

Name: Rico
Rank: Quartermaster
Expertise: Demolitions
and weapons expert,
gear supply
Status: Active

Rico doesn't speak much. But what he doesn't say with words, he says with a well-placed explosive or flamethrower blast! Oh yeah! This penguin is excellent in a tussle, often going crazy on the enemy. He has real flippers of fury and we affectionately call him our squad's "world-class psychopath."

More importantly, Rico packs more than just a punch; he packs all the gear for the entire squad. With our supplies safely stowed in his stomach of steel, he can regurgitate any weapon or piece of equipment in a moment's notice. While Kowalski throws out several options during a tight situation, Rico throws *up* the tools to carry out those very plans!

Distinguishing Marks:

A battle scar marks the left side of Rico's face. How he received it is highly classified.

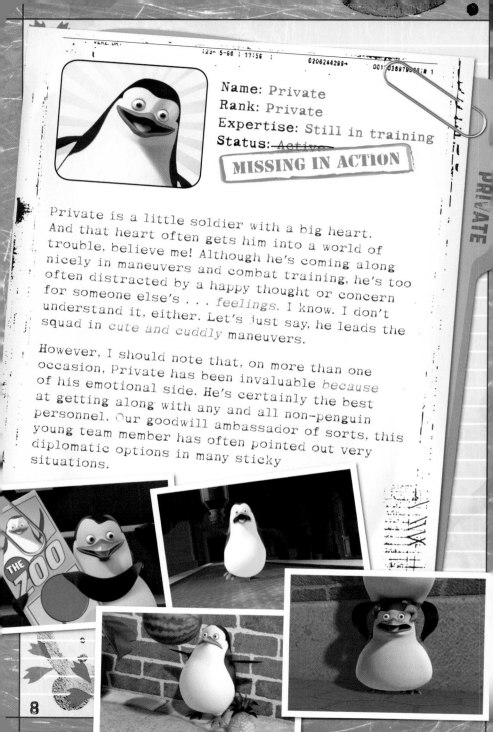

Name: Private
Rank: Private
Expertise: Still in training
Status: ~~Active~~

MISSING IN ACTION

Private is a little soldier with a big heart. And that heart often gets him into a world of trouble, believe me! Although he's coming along nicely in maneuvers and combat training, he's too often distracted by a happy thought or concern for someone else's . . . *feelings.* I know. I don't understand it, either. Let's just say, he leads the squad in *cute and cuddly* maneuvers.

However, I should note that, on more than one occasion, Private has been invaluable *because* of his emotional side. He's certainly the best at getting along with any and all non-penguin personnel. Our goodwill ambassador of sorts, this young team member has often pointed out very diplomatic options in many sticky situations.

SKIPPER'S LOG

07:30 HOURS:

PRIVATE MISSED ROLL CALL. HE'S NEVER MISSED ROLL CALL BEFORE. I ORDERED A COMPLETE AND EXTENSIVE SEARCH OF INTERIOR BASE.

07:31 HOURS:

COMPLETE AND EXTENSIVE SEARCH NOW . . . COMPLETE. UNFORTUNATELY, IT TURNED UP NADA, ZERO, ZILCH. PRIVATE IS NOWHERE TO BE FOUND.

TIME TO GO TOPSIDE!

07:32 HOURS:

COMMENCED COMPLETE AND EXTENSIVE SEARCH OF EXTERIOR PERIMETER.

CHECKLIST

- [x] Cement imitation iceberg
- [x] Pool
- [x] Bucket of fish

07:34 HOURS:

WE SEARCHED THE AREA AND PRIVATE WAS STILL UNACCOUNTED FOR. RICO EVEN RATTLED PRIVATE'S FOOD BOWL. NOTHING HAPPENED.

"FISH AND CHIPS, MAN!" I SHOUTED. THE SUBTLE SOUNDS OF THOSE SUPPLE, SLIPPERY FISH SHOULD'VE BROUGHT THAT PENGUIN SLIDING IN FAST.

NO, PRIVATE WAS DEFINITELY M. I. A. I SUSPECTED ~~FOWL~~ PLAY.
                        foul

07:35 HOURS:

I ASKED KOWALSKI FOR OPTIONS. HE WHIPPED OUT HIS CLIPBOARD AND SKETCHED A FEW POSSIBLE SCENARIOS.

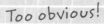

Too obvious!

No way. Bigfoot is just a myth. Yet, I wouldn't rule out the lesser-known myth—Bigfoot's brother-in-law, Stinkfoot.

Highly unlikely but possible just the same. I've never trusted that lady of the loch.

07:40 HOURS:

RICO HACKED UP THE BINOCULARS AND I SCANNED THE PARK. NO SIGN OF OUR YOUNGEST RECRUIT.

KOWALSKI SKETCHED A "MISSING" FLYER. I THINK HE CAPTURED THE SOLDIER'S LIKENESS QUITE WELL.

07:42 HOURS:

KOWALSKI ASKED PERMISSION TO SKETCH TWO HUNDRED MORE FLYERS.

"PERMISSION DENIED!" I REPLIED.

I DECIDED THAT PASSING OUT FLYERS WAS A WASTE OF OUR VALUABLE TIME AND RESOURCES. THIS SEARCH MISSION COULDN'T BE LEFT TO CHANCE. IT CALLED FOR A THOROUGH INVESTIGATION AND, MORE IMPORTANTLY, COVERT SURVEILLANCE. OH, YES. IT WAS TIME TO GET MY FREAK ON FOR RECON!

I ORDERED RICO TO REGURGITATE THE ZOO MAP.

POTENTIAL ENEMIES ON ALL SIDES. IT'S A SOLDIER'S PARADISE!

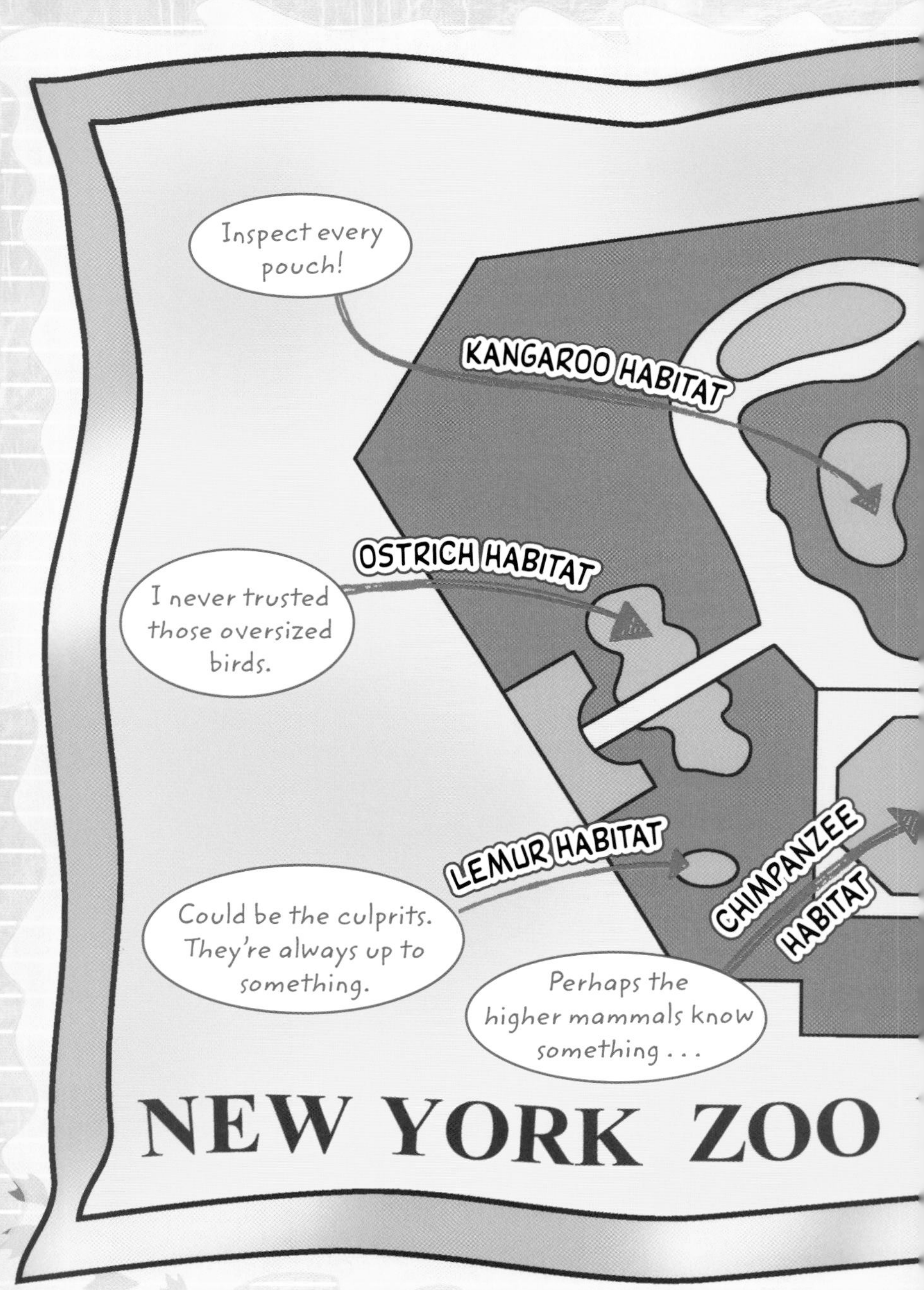

NOTE: Next time let the map dry before placing it in the logbook.

07:50 HOURS:

WE PERFORMED A COVERT BELLY-SLIDE TO MARLENE'S HABITAT. WE LANDED IN OUR STANDARD, REGULATION KARATE STANCE.

"KOWALSKI, RICO, SECURE THE AREA!" I ORDERED. "I'VE HAD ONE GOOD SOLDIER GO MISSING TODAY. YOU NEVER KNOW WHO'LL BE NEXT."

MARLENE COMPLAINED THAT, ONCE AGAIN, WE DIDN'T KNOCK. AS WE'VE EXPLAINED BEFORE, SUCH PLEASANTRIES ONLY SLOW US DOWN. WE PRIDE OURSELVES ON OUR RAPID RESPONSE.

MARLENE HAS PROVEN TO BE FRIENDLY IN THE PAST. BUT CAN SHE TRULY BE TRUSTED? LUCKILY, WE KEEP EXTENSIVE FILES ON CIVILIAN PERSONNEL, AS WELL.

Name: Marlene
Species: Otter
Friend or Foe: Friend

Marlene the otter is new to our zoo and has since become an ally to the squad. She's friendly, playful, and even quite helpful at times. Unfortunately, she can be a bit naïve when it comes to the ways of military strategy. Marlene doesn't always see the importance of a covert rendezvous or stealthy recon missions.

Marlene is unique in the fact that she has more patience for some of the zoo's more annoying residents. Although she does have her breaking point, this easygoing otter has often mediated disputes between our squad and other zoo occupants. Those hapless creatures don't know just how lucky they are.

07:57 HOURS:

I ASKED KOWALSKI FOR OPTIONS. HE SUGGESTED WE INTERROGATE MARLENE AS TO PRIVATE'S WHEREABOUTS.

"AGREED," I REPLIED. IT DIDN'T MATTER THAT SHE WAS FRIENDLY IN THE PAST. IN A SITUATION LIKE THIS, EVERYONE IS A SUSPECT.

07:58 HOURS:

MARLENE TOLD US THAT SHE HADN'T SEEN PRIVATE. I MUST ADMIT I WAS DISAPPOINTED. I HAD HOPED THE INTERROGATION WOULD'VE GONE BETTER.

08:00 HOURS:

I ORDERED THE MEN TO SEARCH HER HABITAT. EVEN THOUGH PRIVATE WASN'T THE BEST AT CAMOUFLAGE AND STEALTH, HE HAD BEEN *TRAINED* BY THE BEST—ME!

MARLENE COMPLAINED, CLAIMING WE WERE "RANSACKING" HER HOME. I DIDN'T KNOW WHAT SHE MEANT BY THAT. BUT IF RANSACKING MEANT WE WERE CONDUCTING A THOROUGH SEARCH AND INSPECTION OF HER DOMICILE, THEN RANSACK WE DID.

08:05 HOURS:

RICO REMOVED A THROW RUG REVEALING A GRATED MANHOLE!

AH, YES, I REMEMBER THAT HOLE WELL . . .

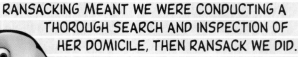

It was a night like any other. We were fast asleep in our bunks when I gave the order to roll over. Then we were ripped from our slumber by a bloodcurdling scream.

Of course, we woke fast and took a defensive stance.

Upon seeing there was no immediate threat, we belly-slid over to the source of the scream— Marlene's habitat.

After careful analysis, we discovered that Marlene had simply screamed because she heard a ghostly moan. That's when King Julien, Maurice, and Mort arrived. Julien insisted on ordering the spooky spirit away with his dancing skills. It was a sight I won't soon get out of my head, believe me.

Of course, later that night, when Marlene heard the spooky sound again, it was *our turn* to probe for that pesky poltergeist. "All right, boys," I said. "Commence Operation Our Turn!"

This time we stayed in Marlene's habitat as she went back to sleep. We soon found out that the *ghostly noise* was nothing more than Marlene snoring.

The sassy otter admitted she snored but explained that her snoring isn't the sound she heard. Just then, we heard the noise ourselves. It was a deep, ghastly moan.

Kowalski traced it to the grated hatch leading to the sewer below. ----→

Rico coughed up a lit stick of dynamite and I dropped it into the sewer. When the blast blew the grate off the hole, Marlene and I fell through, splashing into the sewer water below. The lid above slammed shut, separating us from the rest of the squad.

I was unconscious in that swirling swill. But somehow, I was still alive. ----→

Marlene took point and we did a little recon. Then the flashlight went out, which was quite unfortunate . . . because we came across a humongous sewer monster!

The beast charged, and during an evasive maneuver, I accidentally pressed a button on the tape recorder. Marlene's snoring ripped out of the tiny speaker like a buzz saw. When the giant beast heard her horrible snore, it made the same ghostly moans we'd heard from above. ---→

I got the flashlight working again to discover that the sewer monster was only a large alligator. Normally, I wouldn't write the word *only* in front of the phrase *large alligator*.

←---ⅉ

However, this cold-blooded beast turned out to be a friendly gator named Roger. And Roger was just as scared of Marlene's snoring from above as she was of his moans below. Mystery solved!

SKIPPER'S LOG

AFTER REVIEWING MY FILE, I DECIDED THAT MARLENE COULD BE TRUSTED AND WASN'T RESPONSIBLE FOR PRIVATE'S DISAPPEARANCE. IF I EVER FIND MYSELF IN THE SWIRLING CURRENTS OF RAW SEWAGE AGAIN, I'D WANT HER BY MY SIDE.

08:31 HOURS:
I CALLED RICO'S NAME. HE HOCKED UP A SMOKE BOMB TO COVER OUR ESCAPE. MARLENE COUGHED AS WE VANISHED IN THE HAZE.

08:32 HOURS:
WE BELLY-SLID DOWN THE WALKWAY AND ZIPPED TOWARD THE LEMUR HABITAT.

08:33 HOURS:
WE TOOK UP POSITION BEHIND A PALM TREE. KING JULIEN WAS IN HIS USUAL POSITION, SITTING ATOP HIS BAMBOO THRONE.

EVERYTHING LOOKED QUIET . . . TOO QUIET. JULIEN WORE HIS USUAL WITLESS EXPRESSION. THAT'S JUST HOW I'D EXPECT HIM TO LOOK IF HE HAD KIDNAPPED OUR COMRADE.

ATOP THE PALM TREE

DOWN THE VOLCANO

INSIDE THE BOUNCE HOUSE

UNDER THE PILE OF FRUIT

BEHIND THE SMOOTHIE BAR

"KOWALSKI," I SAID. "ANALYSIS."

MY SECOND-IN-COMMAND QUICKLY GAVE ME POSSIBLE LOCATIONS WHERE THE LEMURS COULD HAVE STASHED PRIVATE.

KNOW YOUR ENEMY IS WHAT I'VE ALWAYS SAID. IT'S A GOOD THING I KEEP DETAILED FILES ON THE FUZZY-TAILED LOWER MAMMALS, AS WELL.

Name: "King" Julien
Species: Lemur
Friend or Foe: Unknown

KING JULIEN

This annoying ringtail claims he's king of the entire zoo. Although his fellow lemurs believe that crazy claim, we penguins do not! Julien is demanding, arrogant, whiny . . . and those are his good points. However, the lemur isn't *all* bad and would normally be classified as an ally, if he wasn't getting everyone into so much trouble. King Julien isn't the brightest bulb in the box, either. This royal pain believes in so-called sky spirits that grant his every wish. This belief makes him quite vulnerable to anyone hoping to take advantage of his superstitions. Just ask the chimpanzees.

The only thing Ringtail loves more than himself is dancing. He often throws all-night dance parties, keeping the entire zoo awake.

NOTE: We penguins are a resourceful bunch. I've learned to adapt.

Name: Maurice
Species: Lemur
Friend or Foe: Friend

This stout little lemur is King Julien's sergeant-at-arms and right-hand ~~man~~. Maurice is also an official adviser and is often the only voice of reason in the lemur habitat. But that's only when he's not fanning, pampering, or taking orders from his royal hiney-ness.

Maurice rolls his eyes at some of the king's crazy whims (not to Julien's face, of course). He's often skeptical of most new decrees but follows them anyway. He does try his best to steer Julien in the general direction of logic and reason. It's lucky for the entire zoo that Maurice is stationed in the lemur habitat. Otherwise, King Julien would be *completely* out of control.

Name: Mort
Specie: Lemur
Friend or Foe: Friend

Mort is King Julien's biggest fan and most loyal subject. Sad Eyes, as I call him, takes infinite abuse from the king in exchange for merely being in his presence. With his long bushy tail, big watery eyes, and high-pitched voice, Mort is found to be downright adorable by everyone else. Little Mort doesn't seem to notice, though. He only longs for his king's approval.

Mort has an unhealthy attraction to King Julien's feet. There's nothing the little lemur would like more than to spend his every moment cuddling the royal feet. This annoys Julien to no end. The king of the lemurs has gone so far as to make several royal decrees on the subject. Yet, no matter how harsh the punishment, little Sad Eyes can't seem to control himself.

25

08:41 HOURS:

IN A BLUR OF BLACK AND WHITE, WE SOMERSAULTED INTO THE LEMUR HABITAT, TAKING THEM COMPLETELY BY SURPRISE. IT'S WHAT WE DO.

"ALL RIGHT, RINGTAIL," I SAID. "I DEMAND YOU RELEASE OUR MISSING COMRADE!"

KING JULIEN HOPPED DOWN FROM HIS THROWN. "I AM KING," HE SAID. "AND I DEMAND THAT I AM THE ONLY ONE WHO IS MAKING WITH THE DEMANDS!"

"HE'S RIGHT," AGREED MAURICE. "HE *IS* QUITE DEMANDING."

JULIEN WHIPPED OUT A PIECE OF PAPER AND THRUST IT TOWARD US.

KING JULIEN'S OFFICIAL ROYAL KINGLY DEMANDS

(of the day)
(subject to change at any time)
(and then maybe change back again)

1. All gray animals must dye their fur so they don't match mine
2. Snow cone Sundays
3. More groveling! Always more groveling!
4. Never touch the royal feet.

08:45 HOURS:

I HAD THE MEN SEARCH THE HABITAT. NOTHING, KING JULIEN WAS HIS NORMAL, ANNOYING SELF. NOTHING SEEMED OUT OF THE ORDINARY AFTER ALL.

08:47 HOURS:

WE WERE ABOUT TO MOVE ON WHEN MORT GAVE US SOME INTEL. HE CLAIMED TO HAVE SEEN PRIVATE HEADING TOWARD THE CHIMPANZEE HABITAT. INTERESTING.

I'M NOT SURE WHETHER TO TRUST LITTLE SAD EYES. THERE WAS A TIME WHEN THIS LITTLE LEMUR CAUSED US ALL KINDS OF GRIEF. HERE IS THE CLASSIFIED FILE ON THAT INCIDENT . . .

TOP SECRET

King Julien was not happy when he realized the gift shop Mort dolls were becoming more popular than his own Julien dolls. Marlene told him how her dolls had been sent back to the factory for defects.

Ah, yes. I remembered that defect very well. The heads of the little otter dolls would pop off for no reason. It wasn't a selling point, believe me.

The next day, oddly enough, an angry crowd of zoo customers gathered outside the gift shop.

It turned out that all the Mort dolls were being recalled to the factory, as well. It seemed that they had been tainted with some sort of toxic substance. - - - - ->

"A factory recall?" asked Marlene. "Wait a second . . ."

Marlene was right to be suspicious. Something didn't smell right, and it wasn't just the stinky Mort dolls. Just then, Alice the zookeeper walked by, pushing a cart piled high with boxes of the toxic toys. Alice didn't notice the real Mort running along the wall beside her. He jumped into the top box and she unknowingly sealed him inside.

"Sad Eyes!" I shouted as Alice wheeled the box away.

We all marched to the lemur habitat to find out what Julien knew. Marlene was positive he had something to do with the putrid plushes.

"Fine," said Julien. "I was maybe indirectly responsible, in a way that's not my fault, for the recalling of the annoying Mort dolls." It turned out that Julien had all the zoo skunks spray the dolls.

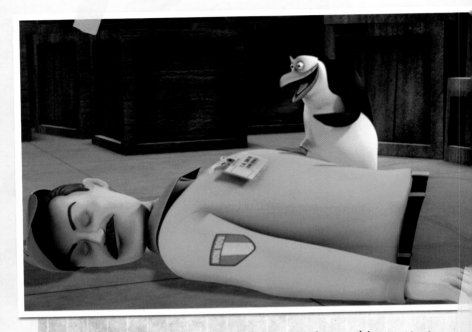

Ringtail didn't seem too concerned until we told him that the real Mort had been shipped out with the dolls. All right, he didn't seem too concerned *after* we told him, either.

I decided to mount a rescue mission to save Sad Eyes. My team and I packed ourselves inside a box being mailed to the factory. Once there, Rico gave a factory worker a well-placed karate chop, and knocked him out cold. We were in! It was time to find Mort.

Suddenly, a nearby box began quaking with more pops than the Fourth of July. Rico coughed up a flamethrower so we could return fire. Then the box burst open revealing Julien lounging in a hammock, popping popcorn. He had shipped himself, too!

Against my initial instincts, I decided to let Julien join the mission. That turned out to be a big mistake. He officially became a hazard to the operation when he accidentally lodged one of his King Julien dolls between two of the factory gears. Sparks flew and guards came running as we hustled Ringtail out of sight.

Our search for Mort ended when we spotted him running on a long conveyer belt. That wouldn't have been so bad, really. It was kind of like running on a treadmill—good exercise. Unfortunately, this moving belt conveyed defective toys to a giant shredder! We jumped onto the conveyer belt and ran alongside Mort as I shouted orders to Kowalski.

"Hit the *kill* switch!" I ordered. Kowalski pressed a button and two giant arms came down and crushed the toys behind us. "Kill the *hit* switch!" I shouted.

That only brought down a giant stamp. And then came a buzz saw, followed by two swinging razor-sharp blades. What kind of toy factory was this?

With Mort holding tight to my head, we desperately held onto the track to keep from falling into the deadly toy shredder. I had one last idea. I turned to Rico. "Surprise me."

Rico hacked up a cinder block and it dropped into the shredder, jamming it up. As it blew apart, gears exploded everywhere. One hit the conveyer belt and shot all of us across the factory. We sailed toward a giant pot of molten metal.

Luckily, we were lassoed by none other than Ringtail himself! That crazy lemur swung over on a giant hook as he held us by a thin rope. We all fell into a box of plush dolls being shipped back to the zoo.

Everything turned out all right . . . except for the part where we brought back a stuffed Private doll instead of Private himself.

"Back to the factory, men!"

SKIPPER'S LOG

MY FILE HELPED ME TO TRUST MORT'S INFORMATION. I DECIDED TO TAKE
SAD EYES AT HIS WORD ABOUT SEEING PRIVATE EARLIER. MORT HAD
GOOD INTENTIONS EVEN IF HE *DID* HAVE A KNACK FOR GETTING INTO
TROUBLE—NOT TO MENTION THAT WEIRD THING WITH KING JULIEN'S
FEET. I REALLY DON'T UNDERSTAND THAT.

AND I HOPE I NEVER WILL.

09:15 HOURS:

WE TOOK UP A SURVEILLANCE POSITION UNDER A PARK BENCH NEAR
THE CHIMPANZEES. I ASKED KOWALSKI FOR AN ANALYSIS.

HE WHIPPED OUT HIS SCANNER. ''SCANNING, SKIPPER,'' HE SAID. HE
AIMED THE DEVICE AT THE HIGHER MAMMALS. ''I'M READING ONLY
TWO LIFE-FORMS. BOTH SIMIAN IN NATURE.''

''LET'S MOVE OUT, BOYS,''
I ORDERED.

09:17 HOURS:

WE BELLY-SLID TOWARD THE
HABITAT, RICOCHETED OFF A
BRICK WALL, AND SPLIT UP. WE
FLIPPED INTO THE CHIMPANZEE
ENCLOSURE FROM THREE
SIDES, LANDING IN PERFECT
FORMATION.

WE TOOK THE CHIMPS
COMPLETELY BY SURPRISE!
JUST THE WAY I LIKE IT.

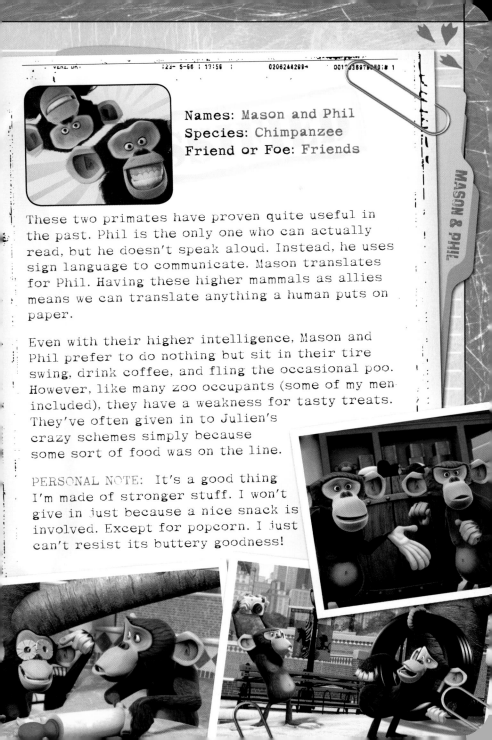

Names: Mason and Phil
Species: Chimpanzee
Friend or Foe: Friends

MASON & PHIL

These two primates have proven quite useful in the past. Phil is the only one who can actually read, but he doesn't speak aloud. Instead, he uses sign language to communicate. Mason translates for Phil. Having these higher mammals as allies means we can translate anything a human puts on paper.

Even with their higher intelligence, Mason and Phil prefer to do nothing but sit in their tire swing, drink coffee, and fling the occasional poo. However, like many zoo occupants (some of my men included), they have a weakness for tasty treats. They've often given in to Julien's crazy schemes simply because some sort of food was on the line.

PERSONAL NOTE: It's a good thing I'm made of stronger stuff. I won't give in just because a nice snack is involved. Except for popcorn. I just can't resist its buttery goodness!

09:20 HOURS:
I BEGAN INTERROGATING THE CHIMPS. THEY KNEW SOMETHING. I WAS SURE OF IT!

PHIL SIGNED AND MASON TRANSLATED. "WHILE I WAS OUT THIS MORNING, SCROUNGING UP A NEWSPAPER (THAT DIDN'T HAVE POO ON IT), PRIVATE CAME BY OUR HABITAT. HE WANTED SOMETHING TRANSLATED." SO FAR, KOWALSKI HAS ONLY BEEN ABLE TO DECIPHER THE FOLLOWING CHIMPANZEE HAND SIGNS.

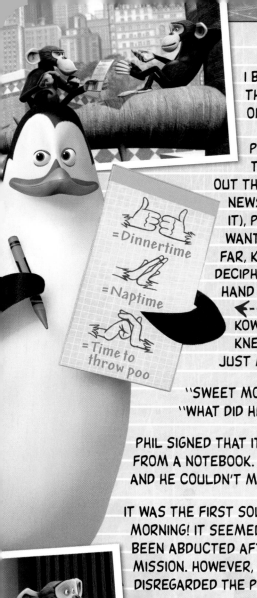

= Dinnertime

= Naptime

= Time to throw poo

KOWALSKI POINTED OUT THAT IF WE KNEW WHAT PRIVATE WANTED READ, IT JUST MIGHT LEAD TO HIS WHEREABOUTS.

"SWEET MOTHER MCARTHUR!" I EXCLAIMED. "WHAT DID HE WANT TRANSLATED?"

PHIL SIGNED THAT IT WAS A PIECE OF PAPER RIPPED FROM A NOTEBOOK. THE HANDWRITING WAS SMUDGED AND HE COULDN'T MAKE IT OUT.

IT WAS THE FIRST SOLID LEAD WE'D GOTTEN ALL MORNING! IT SEEMED THAT PRIVATE HAD NOT BEEN ABDUCTED AFTER ALL; HE WAS ON A SOLO MISSION. HOWEVER, THE YOUNG SOLDIER HAD PLAINLY DISREGARDED THE PENGUIN CREDO: NEVER SWIM ALONE!

WE PENGUINS WERE SUPPOSED TO WORK TOGETHER. IT'S A DANGEROUS WORLD OUT THERE, ESPECIALLY FOR ONE LONE PENGUIN. WHY, EVEN WHEN WE'VE WORKED TOGETHER, WE'VE LOST EVERYTHING WE OWNED . . .

I OPENED UP THE OLD CASE FILE TO REMIND ME OF THE EVENTS OF THAT FATEFUL DAY . . .

TOP SECRET

It all started during a routine training exercise. I split the squad into two teams. It was Rico and Kowalski against Private and me for a little ~~game~~ exercise called Capture the Flag.

After several strategic maneuvers, I was about to get my fins on that very flag. It was almost in my grasp when Julien strolled up and snatched it off the pole. He even blew his nose with it!

I took the now-disgusting flag and tried to explain that this exercise was only for elite forces like ourselves. He wanted to play, anyway, but I informed him of the no civilians allowed policy.

"Are you a penguin or a chicken?" he asked.

I simply ignored him and walked away while he made taunting chicken clucks.

After several days of
obnoxious chicken noises,
I agreed to let him play. It
was the lemurs against the
penguins. If the lemurs won,
they got our TV. If we won,
we got Mort.

- - - - - →

We lined up on the other
side of the zoo and
began the race. After
several covert maneuvers,
Kowalski peeked out from
behind a tree to scan the
flag with his binoculars.

"What if we lose the TV?" asked Private.

"Those lemurs don't have the skills," I replied "But they do have
the flag," said Kowalski.

He was right! Somehow, the
lemurs had won!

As Julien, Maurice, and
Mort slid the TV away
from our habitat, I told
them I wanted a rematch.

Ringtail quickly agreed and
hugged our stereo. "When I
win, this hi-fi will be my-fi!"

I'll be the first to admit that I got somewhat carried away. The lemu kept beating us and beating us and I kept asking for rematch after rematch. I just couldn't accept th fact that we didn't dominate then in such a simple exercise.

Even Kowalski agreed. "No land mammal should be able to move that fast!"

Soon, the lemurs had almost everything we owned. All we had left was a lonely candle to gather around and watch flicker. The TV was much more exciting, believe you me.

It was in our darkest hour when the answer finally came to me. No land mammal should be able to move that fast. That was it! While we had raced across the land, the lemurs traveled over the treetops

We challenged the lemurs to one more game—all or nothing!

As the final game began, I scanned the area and spotted the lemurs leaping through the treetops—just as I suspected.

With soda bottles strapped to our backs and wooden wings fastened to our flippers, we were ready to take to the skies! We hopped up and down, shaking the soda, and then knocked off the caps. We soared over the zoo the way flightless birds only dream of doing.

The lemurs were completely taken by surprise. We buzzed each of our furry foes before capturing the flag and winning the day!

We won all of our equipment back, plus Julien's inflatable bounce house and a new pet named Mort.

REMEMBERING THAT INCIDENT, I REALIZED THAT INSTEAD OF ORGANIZING FLAG-CAPTURING EXERCISES, I SHOULD HAVE BEEN HAMMERING THE PENGUIN CREDO INTO PRIVATE'S SIMPLE BRAIN.

10:00 HOURS:

THE BIG BELL OVER THE MAIN ENTRANCE RANG LOUDLY, SIGNALING ZOO OPENING. THE GATES FLEW OPEN AND HUMANS STREAMED IN.

"GREAT GANDHI'S NUNCHUCKS!" I SHOUTED. "WE'RE STILL ONE MAN SHORT!"

10:01 HOURS:

I ORDERED THE COMMENCEMENT OF OPERATION FAUX FOWL! RICO AND I BELLY-SLID TO THE LEMUR HABITAT. KOWALSKI RETURNED TO BASE TO CRAFT THE DISGUISE.

10:05 HOURS:

THE THREE OF US, ALONG WITH MAURICE, STOOD ATOP OUR SIMULATED ICEBERG. WE WAVED TO THE GATHERING CROWD.

"CUTE AND CUDDLY, MAURICE," I INSTRUCTED. "CUTE AND CUDDLY."

THE PUDGY LEMUR COMPLAINED AS HE SMILED AND WAVED.

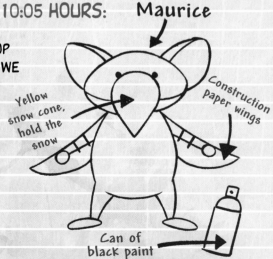

Maurice

Yellow snow cone, hold the snow

Construction paper wings

Can of black paint

TOP SECRET

I QUICKLY REMINDED MAURICE THAT HE OWED US BIG TIME. AFTER ALL HE PUT US THROUGH THAT TIME . . . I OPENED UP THE CASE FILE TO REMIND HIM OF THE TIME HE LED US ASTRAY.

The boys and I were enjoying a little R & R when suddenly, maniacal laughter filled the air.

"I didn't know we had a hyena exhibit at the zoo," said Private.

"We don't," I replied. ⌐----➤

With that, we zipped out of our base and sprang into action. We took cover as Alice the zookeeper walked by carrying a small crate with Julien inside. He looked crazier than usual. His eyes were red and he cackled a horrible maddening laugh.

We slid over to the lemur exhibit to investigate. Maurice reported that, one minute, Julien was sitting on his throne, eating red lychee nuts. And the next minute, he was laughing like crazy. It sounded like business a usual to me. But Maurice assured us that Julien was loonier than normal.

I suggested Maurice replace Julien as king until he recovered. He agreed, but only until Julien returned from the infirmary. ----➤

Maurice decided to take the royal throne for a test drive. He gobbled down some of Julien's lychee nuts.

It all went downhill after that. Maurice quickly declared himself king and ordered the rest of the zoo animals to swear their undying loyalty to him. Well, that's where I draw the line! ----→

←----

Maurice tried to enforce his rule by cutting power to the zoo. Coincidentally, the zoo's control room was located under the lemur habitat. A little too coincidentally, if you ask me. But that was another puzzle for another time. Right then and there, we had to go in and we had to do it quickly.

In no time, Rico regurgitated a lit stick of dynamite and we blew in the door to the control room. The trouble is, we were soon snared by Maurice and his two gorilla henchmen—Bada and Bing.

Believe me, those giant primates don't look any prettier upside down.

Luckily we escaped before the gorilla goons could damage more than our pride. So we made our way to the hospital—it was time to investigate the original crazy king.

After careful analysis, Kowalski discovered that bad lychee nuts made the lemurs . . . nuts. The only way to reverse the effects of the tainted berries was some of Julien's guava berry milkshake.

Julien had gone through several guava berry shakes and was back to normal. He didn't seem to care that Maurice had cut the power to the entire zoo. He was only outraged that Maurice had eaten his lychee nuts.

Kowalski created a spray version of the shake and we set off to stop Maurice.

Back at the lemur domain, my squad tangled with the two big apes while Julien went to spray Maurice with the antidote. Unfortunately, Ringtail got sidetracked gloating and taunting Maurice. We were all captured before he could turn Maurice back to normal.

Lucky for us, little Mort had enough guts to grab the spray bottle himself. He gave Maurice a face full of guava berry juice and turned him back to normal.

Maurice was embarrassed by his actions and barely remembered a thing. Everything went back to the way it was. That is, until Mort found the lychee nuts. But that is another report altogether.

TO BE FAIR, MAURICE *HAD* BEEN UNDER THE INFLUENCE OF LYCHEE NUTS THAT DAY. I SUPPOSED WE COULD TRUST HIM NOW.

10:30 HOURS:

I EVALUATED MAURICE'S PENGUIN DISGUISE. HE WAS CLOSE TO CUTE BUT BARELY APPROACHING CUDDLY. FORTUNATELY, HIS ACT WAS GOOD ENOUGH TO FOOL THE ZOO PATRONS. AND THERE WEREN'T ANY LYCHEE NUTS NEARBY TO SABOTAGE OUR MISSION.

11:00 HOURS:

FINALLY, THE CROWDS BEGAN TO THIN.

"WHAT IS THE MEANING OF THESE THINGS?" ASKED A FAMILIAR ANNOYING VOICE. IT WAS KING JULIEN. HE AND MORT LEAPED INTO OUR HABITAT.

"IT IS PAST TIME FOR MY MORNING PAMPERING," SAID THE LEMUR. "AND I AM MISSING A MAIN PAMPERER FROM MY PAMPERING POSSE."

I WAS ABOUT TO GIVE THAT LEMUR AN EARFUL WHEN KOWALSKI POINTED TO THE GIFT SHOP.

"ALICE AT THREE O'CLOCK!" HE SHOUTED.

THE ZOOKEEPER WAS HEADED OUR WAY.

Name: Alice the zookeeper
Species: Human
Friend or Foe: Foe (except during feeding time)

Alice is one of the crankier zoo overlords. In fact, she's a riddle wrapped in mystery and dipped in nasty sauce. Always irritable, she stomps around the zoo and can dish out grouchiness at any moment. Lucky for us, she seems more annoyed at the zoo customers than the zoo inhabitants.

I'll give this to Alice: She's the only human that suspects there's more to us penguins than meets the eye. She glares at us suspiciously every chance she gets. It certainly keeps us on our toes. That makes her a worthy adversary and I appreciate that. I'll never forgive her for enforcing the "do not feed the animals" rule. But I admire her just the same.

DO NOT FEED THE ANIMA

11:05 HOURS:

WITH LIGHTNING-FAST REFLEXES, I SLAPPED JULIEN OFF THE PLATFORM AND INTO THE POOL SO ALICE WOULDN'T SEE HIM. KOWALSKI TRIED TO DO THE SAME TO MORT BUT THE LITTLE LEMUR THOUGHT WE WERE PLAYING A GAME. HE KEPT BOUNCING UP AND DOWN, STAYING JUST OUT OF KOWALSKI'S REACH.

ALICE WAS GETTING CLOSER SO I SHOUTED RICO'S NAME. HE BENT OVER AND SWALLOWED MORT WHOLE.

"OOH, I LIKE DARK AND SLIMY!" SAID MORT'S MUFFLED VOICE. "AND POPCORN! YAY!"

RICO'S STOMACH INVENTORY (SHORT LIST)

BINOCULARS	FLASHLIGHT	SARDINE TINS
CROWBAR	FLAMETHROWER	PLAYING CARDS
TIME BOMB	ZOO MAP	RADIO
CANNONBALL	FISHING POLE	ROPE
BOWLING BALL	TNT	HAMMER
BALL BEARINGS	POPCORN	MORT
BASEBALL BAT	FISH	

11:06 HOURS:

ALICE EYED US SUSPICIOUSLY. AFTER A MOMENT, THE DISTRUSTING ZOOKEEPER CONTINUED DOWN THE SIDEWALK.

11:08 HOURS:

JULIEN CLIMBED OUT OF THE POOL AND SPIT OUT A LONG STREAM OF WATER. HE DEMANDED THAT WE RETURN HIS WORSHIPERS. RICO REGURGITATED MORT, AND MAURICE THREW DOWN HIS FINS AND BEAK. THE LEMURS STORMED OFF. WE WERE STILL A MAN SHORT, BUT AT LEAST THERE WERE NO MORE CIVILIANS TO COMPROMISE THE MISSION.

I'VE SAID IT BEFORE AND I'LL SAY IT AGAIN—STAY AWAY FROM THE LEMURS. THEY'RE NOTHING BUT TROUBLE. ONCE WE TRIED TO GET VERY FAR AWAY FROM THOSE MADDENING MAMMALS ... AND ALMOST SUCCEEDED. HERE IS THE CLASSIFIED FILE ...

TOP SECRET

It all began one night when we awoke to find our fuzzy-tailed neighbors raiding our refrigerator.

"Those snack provisions are for authorized personnel only!" I shouted

"It is only I, King Julien," he said, "wh is borrowing your delicious food for my stomach."

Apparently that wasn't annoying enough. That lousy lemur interrupted our morning calisthenics by knocking golf balls into our habitat. And to top it off, the lemurs entered our base at all hours, without knocking I might add, simply to watch our television. "You're out of juice," said Mort.

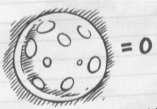 = 0

I'd had enough! We needed a vacatior I wanted a destination with a lemur population of zero. Kowalski narrowe it down to one place—the moon.

Kowalski built a rocket ship and Rico coughed up some dynamite to pile under it for thrust. We put on our space helmets and got in.

"Is it safe?" asked Private.

"Technically speaking . . . maybe," replied Kowalski.

With Kowalski at the controls, we blasted off and soared into the foggy sky. Our trip was short, and we soon skidded to a stop on the moon's surface. We explored the hazy lunar landscape while Kowalski took readings.

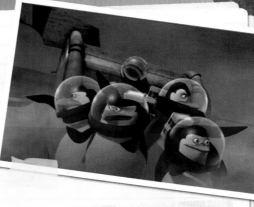

"Oxygen content . . . surprisingly high," he reported. "Moon cheese content . . . disappointingly low."

We quickly discovered that we weren't alone on that rock. We ran into an alien life-form that was oddly catlike. He was a cat who lived on the moon. I called him Mooncat!

Mooncat was quite excited to see us. He was so excited, in fact, that his mouth watered when he invited us to dinner.

We journeyed to his humble dwelling where he offered to put Private into his teleportation machine. It was a teleportation machine that looked oddly like a microwave.

"Camouflage," I said. "I like that!"

In the end, I was deeply touched by Mooncat's generosity. Here we were, four strangers to his world and he opened up his home to us. Even though the moon is far away, he treated us quite neighborly.

It made me think I was a bit hasty trying to get away from our lemur neighbors. I vowed to return to Earth and give myself an attitude adjustment.

Mooncat didn't want us to go. He was so upset that his stomach grumbled. Fortunately, I ordered Rico to regurgitate a tin of sardines. Mooncat was quite grateful for the gift. He waved good-bye as we strapped ourselves into our rocket and blasted off.

We hurtled back toward the zoo, aimed at the pool around our base. "Prepare for splashdown," said Kowalski.

Due to a slight miscalculation, we ended up in a crashdown instead. As we climbed from the wreckage, we spotted the lemurs pushing our television toward their habitat.

Normally, I would have been furious. But thanks to the fine example of hospitality from our new friend, Mooncat, I decided to let it go. I turned to look up at the glowing moon in the sky. Instead, I saw the "mooncat" waving from atop a nearby building. "Bye!" he shouted. "Thanks for the fish!"

I glared at Kowalski. "So, we didn't go lunar?"

He whipped out his clipboard. "It seems I forgot to carry the two." Since there was no such thing as mooncat hospitality, I didn't feel quite so neighborly anymore. It was time for Operation Hammerhead.

"Hammer whose head, exactly?" Julien asked nervously.

Rico coughed up a hammer and the lemurs took off running.

SKIPPER'S LOG

IF THAT FILE PROVED ONE THING, IT'S THAT THE LEMURS ARE WITHOUT A DOUBT THE PESKIEST ZOO ANIMALS.

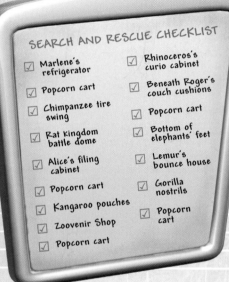

SEARCH AND RESCUE CHECKLIST

- ☑ Marlene's refrigerator
- ☑ Popcorn cart
- ☑ Chimpanzee tire swing
- ☑ Rat Kingdom battle dome
- ☑ Alice's filing cabinet
- ☑ Popcorn cart
- ☑ Kangaroo pouches
- ☑ Zoovenir Shop
- ☑ Popcorn cart
- ☑ Rhinoceros's curio cabinet
- ☑ Beneath Roger's couch cushions
- ☑ Popcorn cart
- ☑ Bottom of elephants' feet
- ☑ Lemur's bounce house
- ☑ Gorilla nostrils
- ☑ Popcorn cart

17:00 HOURS:
THE ZOO FINALLY CLOSED AND THERE WAS STILL NO SIGN OF PRIVATE. WE SCOURED THE REST OF THE ZOO.

17:01 HOURS:
I OFFICIALLY DECLARED PRIVATE MISSING IN ACTION.

17:02 HOURS:
COMFORTED RICO WITH A PAT ON THE BACK.

17:03 HOURS:
TOLD KOWALSKI TO BE STRONG.

17:05 HOURS:
I ORDERED KOWALSKI AND RICO TO POST FLYERS ALL OVER THE ZOO FOR A REPLACEMENT. AFTER ALL, WE WERE A FOUR-MAN TEAM AND A GOOD LEADER KNOWS WHEN TO MOVE ON.

17:06 HOURS:
HAD A WAVE OF SADNESS OVERTAKE ME. I . . . TRIED HARD TO KEEP IT AT BAY. BUT NOTHING WORKED. I KEPT THINKING OF PRIVATE AND HOW DIFFICULT IT WOULD BE TO REPLACE HIM. SURE, HE WAS YOUNG . . . AND GREEN AROUND THE GILLS. BUT I REMEMBER A FINE EXAMPLE OF HIS UNIQUE SKILLS . . .

I OPENED UP THE CASE FILE TO REMINISCE FOR A MOMENT ABOUT MY DEAR FRIEND . . .

TOP SECRET

CASE # 111
PATERNAL EGG-STINCT

Marlene wanted to meet us at the Zoovenir Shop for reasons unknown. We covertly infiltrated the building and assessed the situation before making our presence known.

It turned out she just wanted to tell us about an egg she found in her habitat.

Marlene informed us that back at her old aquarium, the daddy penguins handled egg duty.

"We are an elite force," I explained. "Not nursemaids." - - - - - →

Male penguins really do handle incubation in the wild. But we can't give in to every gushy urge that nature has burdened upon our species. Unfortunately, the rest of my team was already making goo-goo faces at the tiny egg.

I was about to refuse this daddy mission altogether. But then King Julien and the lemurs burst out of hiding. Ringtail wanted the egg as an heir to his throne. He vowed to raise him to be just like the king himself— handsome, brilliant, and humble.

"We'll take him," I told Marlene.

When we returned to the base, I divided the egg-sitting duty into shifts. The egg would have round-the-clock supervision and training. By the time that rookie hatched, he'd be ready for action!

Right from the get-go, Private didn't seem happy about how the rest of the team handled the egg. He seemed overly concerned when I ran the egg through a dangerous obstacle course. Then Private got upset at Kowalski for trying to increase the egg's IQ through the use of harmless high voltage. And Private was downright beside himself when he caught Rico flying the egg high over the zoo with a kite. He thought we were all pushing it too hard.

I tried to explain to Private that he was just a boy himself. He was a dreamer. What could he know about raising an egg? To prove me wrong, he showed us just what he could do. He nurtured that egg night and day, carried it on his feet (the way civilian penguins do), and cared for it.

Unfortunately, Private momentarily let his guard down and Julien switched the egg for a coconut with Mort inside.

The pesky lemur stood on the sidewalk gloating. That was when the egg was knocked from his hands and went rolling through the zoo.

Of course we sprung into action. We just didn't spring fast enough. We lost the egg somewhere in the crowd.

Private felt horrible. He blamed himself for losing the egg and putting it in danger. However, we spotted the egg running across the sidewalk. Its legs had pushed through the bottom of its shell! Private took the initiative. He led the team in recapturing the egg just before it was about to be smashed by a rogue popcorn cart.

After Private's daring rescue, the egg hatched and out popped a tiny duckling.

Private was thrilled until the mother duck showed up. She was grateful for our care and thanked us for watching the egg. Private hugged the duckling one last time before he went away with his mother.

I could sense a wave of emotion coming on so I told the men to think of something manly like monster trucks.

That night, I told Private how proud I was of him. Private hoped that little duckling would remember us.

Little did we know that in the duck habitat, that little duckling took command. It seemed as if we had rubbed off on that little soldier after all. "Cute and cuddly, boys," said the duckling. "Cute and cuddly."

I WANT YOU!

(MAYBE . . . POSSIBLY . . .
ONLY IF YOU'RE GOOD ENOUGH)

TO BE THE NEWEST MEMBER OF
THE PENGUIN ELITE COMMANDO SQUAD!

I CLOSED THE FILE. I SURE MISSED THAT CUTE AND CUDDLY LUG.

17:40 HOURS:
I EXAMINED ONE OF KOWALSKI'S FLYERS.

I WONDERED IF PRIVATE'S REPLACEMENT WOULD BE UP FOR THE TASK. WOULD THE NEW TEAM MEMBER COME WITH THE RIGHT AMOUNT OF COMPASSION, LIKE PRIVATE HAD FOR THE EGG? OR BE ABLE TO TAKE THE LEAD AS PRIVATE HAD DURING THE EGG'S RESCUE? THE VERY IDEA SEEMED PREPOSTEROUS. I DIDN'T THINK ANYONE WOULD TRULY BE ABLE TO WADDLE IN PRIVATE'S FOOTSTEPS.

17:45 HOURS:
OUR VERY FIRST APPLICANT ARRIVED. "MIND IF I TRY OUT FOR THE JOB?" ASKED THE APPLICANT.

IT WAS PRIVATE!